COUNTERMELODY

A SECOND CHANCE ROMANCE

KARAOKE DIVAS
BOOK 1

NIKKI WREN

AUTHOR NOTE

The following story is a second chance romance that contains explicit, consensual sex scenes. Below you can find a list of content notes so that you may best judge if this is the story for you.

Content Notes for Countermelody:
Drinking of alcohol, brief mention of homophobia, public sexual acts, explicit sexual acts, use of sex toys, and karaoke.

ONE

Weddings were the worst. Wedding speeches were the *absolute* worst.

Especially rambling twenty-minute-long speeches given by the Father of the Groom about fishing of all things. How fishing pertained to his son getting married, Allie had no clue.

"Weddings are the woorrrsssst," Kaden said, mirroring the thoughts in Allie's head.

"Hush!" Allie swatted at his shoulder.

Her best friend stifled a chuckle, draped his arm across the back of her chair, and leaned over. "This is worse than Mrs. Glenrose's social studies class. That woman had a voice that could lull an insomniac to sleep."

"Keep your own voice down," Allie whispered. "And didn't you play Snake on your calculator all through that class?"

"Oh yeah. I beat that sucker like three times. I assume if I pull my phone out, you're going to try and confiscate it just like Mrs. Glenrose, huh?" Kaden leaned over and speared a piece of overcooked chicken from her plate.

She'd learned early in their friendship to just order extra food. He always claimed it tasted better when snatched from someone else's plate.

"Yep." Allie scraped the last of her chicken onto his cleaned plate. "You hate your phone. What would you even do with it?"

"Play Snake. Duh." His grin was wide.

Allie couldn't help but let out a little laugh. "Sorry. You'll just have to suffer with me."

He frowned down at the chicken, poking it with his fork. "How did I let you talk me into being your plus one again?"

"It's not my fault you were an idiot and said yes."

His huff of frustration ruffled the limp curls near Allie's ear and she suppressed a little shiver. "All right, fine. That's on me. But I thought you said your parents were going to be here?"

Allie looked around their table. Of course, they'd been seated at the very back of the banquet room. There were only two other occupants beside Kaden and herself, and the other couple were currently turned to face the speaker. Now the father of the groom was talking about competitive fishing? That was a thing?

"Mom got invited to a conference in Budapest. Something about early detection of some disease or another in the brain scans of chimps." Her mom loved to share her work as a well-respected neuroscientist, and Allie loved listening to her enthusiasm, even if she didn't actually understand most of it.

"And, of course, your dad couldn't pass up tagging along."

"Nope. He plans to eat his weight in rétes and cabbage rolls—"At Kaden's look of confusion, she explained, "Basically a Hungarian strudel."

"That's too bad. I was hoping to see them. The last time was the summer after high school graduation, right?"

"They send their apologies and love." Her parents had always adored her best friend, but Allie and Kaden had drifted apart after Kaden had chosen to go to MIT for college. Sure, the two kept in touch with the occasional text or random gif or meme, but this was the first time they'd seen each other in years. Between Kaden taking internships with various software companies and Allie doing a year abroad in England, their schedules had never matched up. But here they were, both home for a visit and stuck at her second cousin Brandi's (always with an *i*, mind you) wedding.

Her inattention to the speech wasn't helped by the fact that Kaden hadn't moved from where he hovered next to her. She could feel the fabric of his suit jacket where it touched her bare shoulders. It also didn't help that he looked damn good in a suit. When had Kaden's shoulders gotten so broad? He'd let his dark hair grow out a bit at the top but kept the sides short. It looked good on him.

Allie didn't want to think about how good her best friend looked. Ex-best friend? Still a friend, though. Friendships after high school were complicated. Especially when those friends smelled as good as Kaden did.

"Seriously, how long can this man talk about fishing? Do you think this is his way of telling everyone he has a fish fetish?"

Allie's fork clattered to her plate. The man at the other side of the table—what was his name? They'd definitely introduced themselves before the speeches started. Whatever his name was, he threw a concerned look their way, but when she smiled and waved apologetically, he went back to watching the groom's father, who was now pantomiming fighting to reel in a stubborn whopper of a fish.

"You're terrible. Hush, you." Allie tried to swat at Kaden's leg, but he caught her hand in his.

His palm was warm as it wrapped around hers and her breath hitched in her chest. Almost without conscious thought, she stroked her thumb up the side of his. The touch was slow and sensual and unlike how she'd ever touched Kaden before.

A part of her wanted to jerk her hand away and pretend it had never happened, but he tightened his grip on her hand before maneuvering their joined hands to Allie's thigh. His thumb slowly stroked along her palm. His hand pressed against hers, caressing, exploring. Allie could have removed her hand at any point, but she didn't. Her entire being was focused on how he gently slipped his fingers between hers in a move that felt nearly obscene for all its innocence. Everywhere he touched, desire blazed through her. As if he weren't touching her hand at all, but showing her just how he'd touch other parts of her.

A smattering of forced laughter reminded her where they were.

"Kaden," she hissed. "What are you doing?"

"Eyes on the fish-lover, Allie." His hand left hers, but it wasn't relief she felt; it was disappointment. Then strong fingers stroked her knee. "Say the word and I'll stop, and we'll never speak of this again. Promise. We'll go back to being bored by the man who clearly spends more time with fish than his own wife."

His hand didn't move from her knee, but his fingers slid up the inside of her leg. And, God help her, she widened them in response. Just a little.

"Nod, if you agree."

Her mother had given her countless lectures over the

years on "proper guest etiquette" and how to be a nice young woman, and what was currently happening was nowhere near the realm of either of those. They were at a wedding, for Christ's sake. There were people everywhere. This was her best friend, Kaden. When had he gotten so bossy? And why did she like it so much?

She knew she shouldn't. She should say "no" and they could go back to being the comfortable friends they'd always been. All she had to do was shake her head and they could pretend this had never happened. Kaden always kept his word. It had been one of the constants in her life.

Allie gave a sharp, quick nod.

"That's my girl." She could feel his smile against the side of her head as his hand worked its way up the inside of her leg, stroking and pressing and gliding against her skin.

"I haven't told you how good you look in this dress, have I?"

Allie's pulse climbed in time with Kaden's hand as it skirted the edge of her hem and ducked underneath. When his fingertips brushed the edge of her panties, he let out a soft groan that shot straight to her core.

"Just gorgeous. The way it hugs your ass—perfect."

Kaden, sweet Kaden, who she used to stay up all night playing video games with, had a filthy mouth. How had she not known Kaden had a filthy mouth?

His fingertip toyed with the edge of her panties, sliding up and down the crease in her thigh. A small whine escaped her and she brought her hands up to clasp them in front of her mouth.

"You always were terrible at being patient."

She had to strain to hear his barely whispered words even as his fingers slipped under the silky fabric and he cupped her pussy.

Oh Jesus! She couldn't help rolling her hips, pressing herself more firmly into his hand. One finger teased her embarrassingly wet slit and it was all Allie could do not to squirm in her chair or flat out beg for more.

Thankfully, his finger slipped inside her and Allie forgot how to breathe.

"Fuck." The word was low and drawn out and contained a world of need. Almost as much as her own. "You feel incredible. Now, let's see how quietly you can come for me, hmm?"

A small whimper escaped her as he slipped his finger into and out of her, going a little deeper each time. When he'd gone as deep as he could, he crooked his finger, hitting a soft place inside her that sent lightning racing up her spine. Her heart pounded in her chest. Tremors shook her thighs. Heat built in her cheeks and lower belly.

The rest of the room could have been on fire and Allie wouldn't have cared when Kaden used his thumb to press her clit, his finger never slowing.

Allie bit her fingers, still clenched in front of her mouth, to keep from crying out as her climax locked every muscle in her body. When it was finally over, she sat there trying hard to get her breathing under control while Kaden gently cupped her.

"Fuck, Allie. You did so good." His mouth was pressed into the hair next to her ear, his words rough and delicious.

The sound of clapping startled Allie out of her post-orgasm haze. Holy shit, were they clapping for her orgasm? Had the whole venue seen her get finger-fucked under the table?!

Her eyes flew open as she sat up straight in her chair. All the other guests were still facing the other side of the room, where the father of the groom was wiping a tear away from his cheek as he handed off the microphone.

Had he actually caught the fish? Had it gotten away? Hell if Allie knew.

Relief flooded Allie's system, turning her insides to goo almost as effectively as Kaden had. Kaden removed his hand from her panties just in time for servers in white shirts to take away their dinner plates and replace them with slices of wedding cake. Heat burned in Allie's cheeks. Someone must have seen. They had to have seen. Hadn't they?

When she glanced at Kaden, she froze. He had on his biggest grin, the one he'd used to give her before throwing her in the lake or crushing her at Mario Kart. Once he knew he had her full attention, he deliberately stuck his finger—the finger that had just been in her—into his mouth. His eyes closed as he slowly, meticulously, sucked it clean. He pulled it from his mouth with a pop and glanced to the other side of the table where, to Allie's mortification, the other couple had turned around again.

"She can't take me anywhere. I just couldn't help myself," Kaden said with a grin.

Allie was going to kill him. With her dessert fork. To his smug face.

The man grinned and swiped a bit of frosting from his own cake. "No worries, sometimes you just have to use your fingers." His partner swatted at his shoulder, mumbling about manners as he licked the frosting from his finger.

"Well said, sir." Kaden leaned over and whispered just to Allie, "Might want to close your mouth. Or at least put a piece of cake in it."

Allie had no good response to that, so she took a bite of cake. The icing was too sweet and the cake was so dry it had the consistency of sand.

Weddings were the worst.

~

Allie had barely gotten back through her door when her phone rang. It was second nature to swipe Accept when she saw who was calling.

"Hi, sweetie!" Her mom's chipper greeting made Allie cringe. Why had she answered?

Locking the door, she said, "Hi, Mom."

"You're not still at the wedding, are you?"

"No, just got home." She kicked off her shoes and put her purse on the table before flopping onto her worn, old couch. "Why?"

"Oh, I was just hoping to talk to Brandi or maybe her mom. Time zones are messing with me again. I'll have to send her a text. So, how was the wedding? Did Brandi look beautiful?"

"The wedding was good. Brandi looked lovely."

"What's wrong, Allie? Did Kaden stand you up?"

Well, shit. "No, Mom. Kaden didn't stand me up. I…I just have a bit of a headache. That's all." The lie felt bitter but necessary on her tongue.

"Oh, sweetie. I'm sorry. Well, I won't keep you. Call me when you're feeling better. But check the time zone before you do."

"Sure, Mom. And you can tell me all about the conference. Give Dad my love."

"Will do. He's currently out on a Walking Street Food Tour. He was so excited this morning; he was practically vibrating. I've got the bottle of tums waiting for him when he inevitably eats too much. Kiss kiss."

"Kiss kiss, Mom."

She hit the end button and leaned her head against the back of the couch. How could she have let Kaden do…that? At a wedding! With her family! Well, all right, it was very distant family who she didn't see often, but still. The point stood. Anyone could have seen. What if they'd been caught? She would have ruined her cousin's wedding, someone would have called her mom to blab, probably Brandi herself, and Allie would forever be known as the family pervert. All because she was a sexual deviant who hadn't had the willpower to say no. Tears of shame pricked at the corners of her eyes.

Ding.

Ding.

Swiping at her eyes, she looked at her phone screen and cringed for the third time in the last ten minutes.

KADEN:

Allie? Are you all right?

You practically ran out of there. Can we talk? About what happened?

Please

Talking about what had happened was the absolute last thing that Allie wanted to do, right after getting her wisdom teeth put back in her mouth just so she could get them extracted again. Why the hell had she nodded? Why did she desperately want to feel his hands on her, *in* her, again? What was wrong with her?!

Ignoring her phone, she took a long, hot shower and got ready for bed, all the while desperately trying to calm down her anxiety-ridden brain. After she'd pulled on clean pjs, she picked up her phone and plugged it into the charger on her nightstand. She couldn't help but notice that Kaden had called her twice and continued to text her, his messages growing increasingly worried, until:

KADEN:

Please, Allie. Let me know you made it home safe

Fuck, please, Allie

The sour tang of a new wave of guilt overrode the minty taste of her freshly brushed teeth. She didn't want him to worry that she was dead in a ditch somewhere, but the thought of talking to him flooded her with embarrassment so heavy it almost nauseated her. She didn't want to talk about what had happened, but she also couldn't let Kaden worry about her like that.

ALLIE:

Home safe. Just tired.

KADEN:

Good. Ok. Thank you for getting back to me.

Get some good sleep

Talk to you tomorrow?

ALLIE:

Sure

After putting her phone done, she climbed into bed and forced herself to take several big breaths. No one had seen what had gone on under the table. Yes, things would be weird with Kaden for awhile. But they'd been friends for years. Kaden knew her better than probably anyone else in the world, besides her parents. They could get through this weirdness. Things could go back to exactly how they'd been before.

At the time, it didn't feel like a lie.

TWO

Twelve Years Later

"I'm just saying you never go out anymore."

Allie rolled her eyes, grateful that she was on the phone with her mother and not on video. Even at thirty-three, she knew it would have gotten her a lecture about "polite behavior."

"I go out plenty, Mom. The girls and I are going to karaoke tonight." She leaned back in her office chair, her eyes going to the window. The view might have only been of the office building next door, but at least she wasn't stuck in windowless cubicle land anymore.

"Going out with your friends is fine and good, but you haven't gone on a proper date in ages."

An exasperated sigh escaped her before she could catch it.

"Allison, your dad and I are worried about you."

"I know." Well, her mom worried about her lack of a

love life. Dad only worried that she was happy and eating enough. "I just got sick of terrible first dates. No one interests me—"

"But if you met someone who did interest you, promise me you'd at least give them a real shot."

"Yes, Mom. Sure, I promise I'll give them a real shot, ok?"

"All right, sweetie." It was reluctant, but her mom knew that was the best she was going to get.

"Look, I have to get going. That big client meeting is in a couple of minutes and I want to go over my slide deck one more time before it starts." The deck was already open on her computer and while she'd been idly clicking it through it while talking with her mom, she really did want to double-check everything, just in case.

"Oh yes, with that big tech firm from California, right?"

"That's the one. I've really got to go. Give my love to Dad."

"Love you, sweetie! I know you'll knock it out of the park. Kiss kiss."

The confidence in her mom's voice brought a smile to Allie's face. "Will do. Love you too." With that, she hung up and pushed her phone to the side.

She clicked through the deck one more time, occasionally stopping to make micro adjustments to spacing or to tweak a word here or there. It was sleek and professional, with just enough information on the slides to be interesting without being overly wordy. Her assistant, Manny, had printed out her speaker notes that morning and she had made a couple updates in red pen.

The calendar invite reminder popped up, letting her know she had fifteen minutes left. She stood up, smoothed out her skirt, and made sure her silk shirt was tucked in properly and not weirdly bunched around the waist. After gathering her laptop, notes, and phone, she headed for the large conference room in which the client meeting was scheduled to take place.

The room was named "Rainier," which was a joke; while it did have a beautiful view of the Sound and the ferries that crossed it, you couldn't actually see the mountain it was named for. It was the very beginning of fall, which meant they were still enjoying mostly warm weather and clear, gorgeous skies.

She set her stuff near the AV hookup at one end of the long conference table and had verified the projector was working when the glass door to the room opened. Standing quickly, she smoothed her skirt once more. Her boss, Simone, led a group comprised of various senior coworkers and the clients.

With her "professional" smile in place, Allie introduced herself to the CEO. "Welcome to Swest Marketing."

Markus was a surprisingly short, good-looking man in his mid to late thirties. His handshake was firm but not overpowering.

"I look forward to your presentation," he said before turning to his other colleagues. "Here, let me introduce you. This is Travis, our CFO. The brains behind the money."

Travis was an older Black man who had sharp eyes behind his thin-rimmed glasses and a kind smile.

"And this is our CTO—"

"Kaden." The word fell out of Allie's mouth like a brick.

There he was, standing in front of her, with a to-go coffee cup in one hand and a look of shocked delight on his face.

"You two know each other?" Markus asked.

While Allie stood there gaping, Kaden said, "We went to school together, but it's been quite a while. Hello, Allie. It's good to see you." He reached out his hand and she automatically shook it. The warmth of his hand in hers broke through her shock.

She gave herself several swift mental kicks. She was a professional, not a little girl anymore. There was nothing she couldn't handle.

"It's good to see you too, Kaden. I didn't realize you were going to be a part of his meeting." Oof. She hoped her statement came off as curious and not accusatory.

"I wasn't originally slated to come, but the president of the company broke her leg while rock climbing last week, so I got asked to fill in last minute."

"Our Kaden would prefer to be left in the office to deal with the developers and the tech. Sometimes it's good for him to get out," Markus said with a friendly pat on Kaden's back.

Kaden let out a self-conscious laugh before giving Allie a small smile that made her heart drop into her stomach with how both familiar and devastatingly handsome it was. Thankfully, before Allie could embarrass herself anymore, Simone called the meeting to order. Allie moved purposefully back to her laptop as everyone else found seats around the table. As Simone gave the introductory talk, Allie shared their presentation on the projector.

She could do this, just twenty-six slides between her and freedom from being trapped in the room with her ex-best friend. The one who'd finger-banged her under the table at her cousin's wedding. She risked a peek down the table. He caught her eye and gave her a smile that made her insides do little flip-flops.

It was the longest twenty-six slides of her life.

~

Halfway through the deck, Simone called a break and Allie beelined it straight back to the safety of her office. She sank into her chair and put her head into her hands.

Of *course* Kaden was the CTO of a major tech company. And of *course*, that major tech company had hired Swest to help with their branding and customer appeal. She'd researched the company extensively for the presentation, but then again, she'd mostly focused on the company's overall brand and their public leadership. The lack of any mention of the CTO on the website or press releases hadn't even registered with her. Kaden had always been private. Even in college, he'd never given in to peer pressure to join social media.

How dare he be even better looking than he was twelve years ago? There was a gravitas to him now, a maturity that was incredibly appealing. It was as though all the cockiness of his youth had transformed into self-assurance backed by knowledge and experience. Somewhere along the line, he'd grown a beard and it wasn't a scraggly, unkempt thing. No, it was trimmed and luscious. Ugh.

Then there was the way he'd popped the top off his coffee, exposing a pile of whipped cream. He'd taken one finger and swiped a bit before putting it in his mouth. The whipped cream reminded her of icing, which reminded her of the wedding reception and how he'd deliberately waited until she was watching before licking his finger clean. The jerk. It couldn't have been a deliberate reminder, could it? Kaden hadn't even been looking at her. Instead, he'd been engrossed in Simone's part of the presentation.

That particular memory always brought a physical reaction with it. Her body couldn't help but heat and ache whenever she thought of how he'd made her come so hard without anyone at that wedding even noticing. The reaction was made worse because the man who had given her the best orgasm of her life had been in the conference room with her, looking like a slice of heaven in a button-up shirt.

Sitting up straight in her seat, Allie opened her laptop and pulled up her work chat. Unfortunately, there were no fires that desperately needed her attention, but there was a very cute picture of someone's new bulldog puppy in the Pets Chat. Allie opened her email and then closed it again. She squirmed in her seat, the friction of the movement both a relief and a new torture. Her mouse clicked to open a web browser and she stared at the little blinking cursor, unable to decide what to type.

Her eyes flicked to the clock. There were still fifteen more minutes until the end of the break. Fifteen more minutes before she'd be back in the room with Kaden and would have to pretend to not know what it felt like to have his fingers stretching her open... Her gaze went to her closed office door. She shut her laptop and drummed her fingers on the lid. The little tap tap tap of her nails was the only sound in the room.

Wouldn't it be better for her to take the edge off before her next meeting? Surely it wouldn't be good to finish up this important client meeting being all hot and bothered like this.

With her heart beating in her throat, she pushed her skirt up her legs. One hand snaked down her panties, the tips of her finger ghosting over her clit. As she'd done hundreds of times before, she pretended the hand touching her wasn't her own, but bigger, a little rougher...like Kaden's. Heat and need built between her thighs as she stifled a whimper. Her eyes flicked to her closed door with a silent reminder to stay quiet. Her fingers stroked her pussy lips. The rational part of her brain knew she shouldn't be doing this, but still she dipped one finger into herself.

Her underwear didn't allow her the freedom she wanted, so she pushed them down to midthigh. Now she could get two fingers inside herself and use her palm to press against her clit. Half-sinking into the chair, she gave herself over to the movement of her hand and the pleasure building as she stroked in and out of herself.

That delicious peak was so close. All she needed was a few more strokes…when someone knocked on the door.

Panic flared through Allie, closing her throat. In a mad scramble, she sat up and used both hands to yank herself as close to her desk as she could get. There wasn't even time to pull her skirt back down before the door opened and the last person she wanted to see walked in.

"Allie," Kaden said before shutting the door. "Can we talk?"

The edge of the desk bit into Allie's stomach, but she didn't dare lean back, even an inch. All she could do was praise whoever had ordered her desk with a front panel so that Kaden wasn't getting a show from where he stood next to the door.

"Um, now's really not the best time."

He ran his hand through his hair, disheveling it. The move was both familiar and alarmingly attractive. "Look, you have to know I didn't set this up on purpose. I didn't even know you were in Seattle until I walked into that conference room."

A little of the tension bled out of Allie's shoulders. "I know that. Really. I was just as surprised as you were. Honestly, it's more my fault. I've been putting this presentation together for weeks and should have looked more closely at the whole senior leadership staff."

"It really is good to see you, Allie," he said as he took a step closer to her desk.

She stiffened once more and held up her hands.

He frowned, a look of profound hurt crossing his face. "I know things with us ended on a…weird note, but I didn't realize we stopped talking because you were afraid of me. I apologize." He turned back to the door, but stopped and said, "Don't worry about having to work with me further. I'll make up an excuse and head back to the hotel."

Guilt and a different sort of panic clawed its way up Allie's throat. "Wait!"

Kaden stopped and turned toward her with a look of wary hope.

"I'm not…*afraid* of you, Kaden."

"Then what, Allie?" He ran his hand through his hair again. "Why are you acting like this?"

A part of her wanted to blurt out the truth, that she'd just been masturbating to thoughts of his fingers deep inside her again. But she couldn't. She hadn't seen or talked to this man in twelve years. He was probably married to a beautiful woman and had a van full of perfect, adorable babies. Not to mention she was working for his company. This was a business relationship. She had to be professional. She would feel much more professional if she could at least pull her skirt down to cover her exposed vagina, but she couldn't figure out a way to do it without making it painfully obvious what was happening.

"Look, it's really not a good time for me. Could we maybe talk about this later?"

Kaden shook his head as he let out an exasperated huff. "You know what? No." He strode toward the desk, leaned over, and planted his hands. "I'm not falling for that line again. We are going to talk about this now."

Allie's eyes went wide with horror as she unconsciously leaned back in her seat, away from Kaden's looming intensity. His eyes trailed down her chest and to her lap, when that slow, mischievous smile that she'd seen so often growing up pulled at his lips.

"Allie, what were you doing when I came in here?"

Her hands had a death grip on the arms of her office chair and her head swung back and forth wildly as she said, "Nothing."

One hand reached and gently caught her chin, forcing her to look him in the eyes. Those warm brown eyes that always saw right through her. Had never once judged her. That she'd missed for so long.

His voice was soft. "No more lies, Allie. Please."

Her heart broke in her chest. Taking a deep breath, she pushed her chair away from the desk, far enough for him to see, well, everything, and covered her face with her hands.

There was a sharp intake of breath and the sound of footsteps. But instead of heading toward the door to alert HR of indecent exposure in the workplace, they rounded the corner of the desk and stopped next to her chair. Fabric rustled and then her chair swiveled to the side.

"Allie, look at me."

The quiet command in his voice cut through her mortification. She lowered her hands and found him crouched down in front of her. Instead of disgust or concern on his face, all she saw was interest. And maybe hunger.

"No lies, now. Before I came in, were you petting this exquisite pussy?"

Heat flared again in her cheeks and while she couldn't make herself say the words, she did nod.

"Good. Were you thinking about my fingers as you fucked yourself?"

She swallowed hard and nodded again and he let out a little groan that sent warmth flooding south once more.

"Did you come?"

She hesitated. The lie was right there on her lips, but she'd lied enough to him and to herself over the years. "No."

"That's a shame. Want me to fix that for you?"

It was such a bad idea—even worse than masturbating in her office. But then he stroked his thumb over her knee, sending a delicious shiver down her spine. Besides, he'd asked her not to lie to him. "Yes, please."

Kaden let out a pleased hum as he ran his hands up her calf, over her knee, slowly up her thighs and stopped to grip the sides of her panties.

"Due to time constraints, I'm not going to be able to enjoy you as thoroughly as I'd like and this beautiful pussy deserves. Pity, but needs must. You will be quiet for me, won't you?"

Allie nodded, biting her lower lip.

"Good girl," he said, his voice low and warm as he slipped Allie's panties down her thighs. She lifted her feet up so he could maneuver them over her heels.

He gently pushed her knees apart and leaned forward. The scruff of his beard scraped along the inside of her thighs. It was both rough and prickly and sent need straight to her core. Her hips shifted and he chuckled, his breath skating over her skin before he pressed his mouth against her.

A small whine escaped her and she covered her mouth with her hand. Pleasure washed through her as he kissed and licked and explored her every fold. His hands came up to grip her hips, pulling her to the edge of the chair so he could better devour her.

"I've been waiting twelve years to taste you again," he murmured before giving her a slow lick that ended with a flick of his tongue on her clit.

His lips closed around her clit, sucking and licking. Her hand tightened over her mouth as her breath turned ragged. He was relentless. Each suck and lick of his talented mouth drove her closer and closer to her peak and then over it.

It was hard and brutal and the fastest she'd ever climaxed before.

Her body quaked and shook as he continued to kiss her through her orgasm, getting lighter and lighter as she came down. She sank into her office chair, her breathing sharp and ragged as she tried to get enough oxygen back into her lungs.

Dreamily, she looked down to find Kaden looking up at her from between her thighs. He stood up and adjusted his hard cock in his dress slacks. Allie couldn't help but wonder what he looked like. What he would taste like on her tongue and the sounds she could wrench from him with her hands and mouth and lips.

Before she gathered the courage to find out, though, he cupped the side of her face. "Just beautiful."

A pleasant warmth filled her chest. Then reality asserted itself. She was in her office. At work. Dread threatened to consume her, to drown her under panic and worry. Someone must have heard.

"Hey. None of that, Allie." His hand gripped her chin, forcing her to look at him. "Please don't spiral on me. Not when you were so perfect for me. No one heard us. No one knows. Only us."

She took a couple of deep breaths before nodding. He was right. There was no commotion outside, just the usual hubbub of folks on video calls, coworkers chatting, and machines beeping. Security wasn't busting in to escort them from the building.

"Ok… yeah."

"There's my girl." Kaden smiled before rummaging through her desk drawers.

She squashed the glow those words ignited in her chest. "What are you doing?"

"Looking for wet wipes. I know you have some in here somewhere," he said as he shut one drawer and grinned at her. "Unless you want me to go back to the conference room with your sweet taste on my beard."

She swatted at his arm before reaching over to the other side of the desk and opening the top drawer. One slot in the wooden organizer contained packets of wet wipes. She handed one to Kaden. As he used it to clean his beard and lips, she straightened her skirt and realized something was missing.

"Where's my underwear?"

"What, these?" He pulled a corner of her panties from his pocket, showing her just a hint of pale lace before shoving it back into his pocket. "Call it payment for services rendered."

She let out a huff of a laugh.

The smirk fell from his face. "Have dinner with me tonight. I promise to keep my hands to myself. I just want to buy you dinner and catch up. Please."

She wanted to say no. It was the safe option. Yes, he had just gone down on her in her office, but that was even more of a reason to say no.

"I'd like that."

Her willpower seemed to evaporate around this man.

That smile. That happy smile she knew so well looked damn good on his older face. When she was younger, she'd always thought it had been too broad for him, a little on the goofy side, but now it suited him perfectly.

Her own answering smile dropped from her lips. "Wait, no. I can't go to dinner with you tonight."

"Why not?" The smile was gone and Allie had a small, irrational desire to say something, anything, to get it back.

"You're having a business dinner with the heads of Swest Marketing."

"That sounds terrible. I'd rather have dinner with you."

"No!" Allie rose from her chair and barely stopped herself from placing her hands on Kaden's chest. "All the bigwigs will be there. You're expected. You can't miss it. It'll be suspicious."

She could tell by the way Kaden had his jaw set he wasn't buying it, so she changed tactics. "Besides, I have plans to go to karaoke with friends tonight."

"When are you going?"

"To karaoke? We're meeting about eight and usually go to ten. It's a weekday after all. You wouldn't want to join us after dinner, would you?"

"I'd love to. Text me the address." He picked up a pen and jotted down a phone number on a Post-it before checking the time on his watch. "The meeting should restart soon. Meet you in there."

He flashed her that damn smile again before leaving her office and closing the door after himself. All the air left Allie's lungs in a whoosh as she flopped back into her chair. The Post-it note on her desk, adorned with Kaden's scribbled phone number, taunted her.

What in the world had she been thinking, inviting him to karaoke? Maybe she could just "forget" to text him the details. But that felt mean and cowardly. And if Allie was honest with herself, she wanted to see him again. She wanted him to meet her friends.

The two-minute warning for the second half of the meeting dinged from her phone. Heaving a sigh, Allie sat up and straightened her skirt. The feeling of air on her damp pussy made her squirm in her seat. Two minutes. Maybe if she hurried, she could at least go clean up in the bathroom before the meeting. If only she had an emergency pair of underwear in her desk, but this situation had never arisen before, and she hoped it wouldn't be a reoccurring event. Even if she had orgasmed harder than she had in years. As she gathered up her laptop and various materials, she couldn't help but think that it was going to be a long, uncomfortable afternoon.

THREE

The Thursday night karaoke group was large enough to need a Medium-sized room instead of their usual Small. The group was seated on couches and comfy chairs, facing a small platform that held the karaoke equipment—a screen for lyrics, a mic, and speakers. Rosie's pale white skin almost glowed in the neon lights as she stood on stage, belting out the chorus to "Love Hurts."

KADEN:

Heading your way.

The message taunted Allie from her phone screen. She tilted back her drink to get to the last watered-down drops of rum and Coke, and the ice collided with her upper lip. The cold, wet surprise made her jump. After pulling up her camera, she used a cocktail napkin to pat away the water droplets and make sure her lipstick had stayed in place.

"Stop fussing. You look great," Grace said, leaning in to shout over the music.

"Thanks." Allie tried to muster up a smile for her well-meaning friend, but it fell short of the mark.

"Is she playing air-flute?!"

The shout-whisper came from a white guy named Dean, Cass's latest guy of the week. He had been quiet and polite when they'd made introductions earlier in the night, but now he was on his third or fourth drink. With each and every one, his volume and obnoxiousness had increased. A clearly embarrassed Cass elbowed him hard in the gut.

Dean curled away from her, protecting his nearly empty glass. "What? It's weird."

Before Cass could hiss at him, light cut through the room from the back. Every head turned, and Allie instantly recognized the backlit silhouette. She stood, smoothing her pencil skirt and cursing herself again for not going home before meeting Rosie and Grace for dinner earlier.

A look of relief crossed Kaden's face as she met him at the door.

"How many rooms did you go into before finding ours?" she asked.

"Third time was the charm," he said with a small laugh. The door closed behind him, sending the room into dim neon once more, and his eyes went to Rosie on the stage. "Air-flute?"

Allie braced herself, wondering what he was going to say next.

"Nice." He gave a little bob of appreciation with his head. The breath whooshed out of Allie in a giggle as she led him around to take a seat next to her on the couch. Silently, she berated herself for worrying. Yes, it had been a long time, but the Kaden she knew wasn't an asshole.

Then again, Dean hadn't seemed like one earlier in the night.

Rosie went back to belting out the last chorus of "Love Hurts" before finishing the song with an exaggerated bow to rounds of applause. She flounced off the small platform —no mean feat considering she was wearing her favorite pair of sparkly combat boots—and threw herself onto one of the small couches. She took a long drink of her beer and stuck her hand out toward Kaden.

"Hiya, I'm Rosie."

He took her offered hand and shook it. "Kaden, high school friend of Allie's. Great job, by the way."

"Why, thank you! Not everyone can appreciate quality air-flute, you know," Rosie replied with a cutting glare towards Dean, who seemed oblivious to the danger he was currently in. Though she looked cute and little, growing up trans in western Washington had meant she'd dealt with more than her fair share of shit and had learned that sometimes the only way to win was to fight fucking dirty. She was the sweetest, toughest woman Allie knew.

Next up, Allie introduced Grace, who had that gleam in her eye that meant Allie was in for an interrogation after the night was over. Grace had inherited her mother's gorgeous long dark hair and slender nose. Tonight's glasses were a pair of black cat eyes with little rhinestones at the points.

Cass leaned over Dean and waved. Despite being a white girl living in the Pacific Northwest, she'd managed to keep her California tan by being outside every minute she could. At five-foot eleven, she was the tallest of their little group.

"Dean," Cass's date said with a nod. "Want a drink?"

Eyebrows drawn together, Cass said, "You sure you should be having any mo—?"

"Pff. It's fine. 'Sides, can't let the new guy drink alone."

Cass looked unconvinced as Dean lurched up from his seat and stared pointedly at Kaden.

"Uh." Kaden looked between Dean, Cass, and Allie. "Sure, I guess. Whatever IPA they have on tap. Thanks, man. Do you want another, Allie?"

"No, I'm good." She had already hit her two-drink limit and worried about what she might say (or do) if she had another one.

After everyone else declined a refill, Dean shrugged and left.

"My turn," Cass called even before the door had fully closed. When the first angry notes of "Killing in the Name" rang out, Allie cringed. It was never a good sign when Cass went back to her angsty high school roots.

Regret washed through Allie for inviting Kaden even as he bobbed his head along with Rage Against the Machine. To be fair, though, their weekly karaoke nights were typically just the four women.

Halfway through the song, Dean returned, handed Kaden his beer, and retook his seat. He took a long sip of what looked like another double whiskey as Cass put a bit too much emphasis on the word *killing* as she sang.

Grace took the next song, Lady Gaga's "Bad Romance," which was one of her favorites. Next up, Dean did a truly cringeworthy rendition of "Blurred Lines." Secondhand embarrassment had Allie squirming in her seat as he slurred the words, nearly slobbering onto the mic.

Her eyes darted to try and gauge Kaden's reaction. When their eyes met, they shared a mutual grimace. A warm arm encircled her shoulders and she gratefully leaned into Kaden's side. On the couch across the way,

Cass slumped as if she were wishing the cushions would swallow her whole.

When the song finally ended, Dean shouted, "Thank you! Thank you!" to a round of lackluster applause. He stumbled back to his seat and planted a sloppy kiss on Cass's bright red cheek.

"Ok, who's next?" Grace asked in an overly cheerful voice. Her gaze locked on Allie. "What about you, Allie? You haven't had a song in a while."

"Um…"

"Come on. Show me how it's done and I'll go after you," Kaden said, giving her shoulder a squeeze.

"All right. All right."

Kaden's hand pressed between her shoulder blades, pushing her up gently but firmly from the couch. Allie forced her locked legs to carry her to the monitor. The list of songs seemed to blur and meld before her eyes. Her mind whirled, trying to find the perfect song to sing. The one that would knock Kaden's socks off. Then she started worrying about how long she was taking to pick a song and just punched a familiar one at random. Turned out she'd picked "Toxic" by Britney Spears. The music started and Allie focused her entire being on the words scrolling across the screen in front of her and the microphone clutched in her hands.

Halfway through the song, her shoulders finally started to inch down from around her ears. The familiar wash of the music, her voice rising and falling with it, was soothing. She'd done this exact thing hundreds of times over the years. During one chorus, she risked a peek at her audience. Dean was hitting his drink hard. The girls were all singing along with her, Rosie was even dancing in her seat, and Kaden's attention was entirely riveted on her. The intensity of his gaze nearly made her stumble over the words. Naked heat and longing were clear on his face and Allie felt warmth cascade from the crown of her head to the tips of her toes in response.

Her muscles went loose and warm. She started swaying her hips in time to the music, rolling them and shimmying along with the music. A tingly thrill crawled up her spine as he watched her hips like maybe they could unravel the mysteries of the universe. It was headier than a shot of tequila on an empty stomach.

The end of the song came too soon. Allie grinned and caught her breath as the room cheered and whooped. Cheeks burning, she put the mic back into its stand and stepped off the platform and almost stumbled into Kaden who had moved toward the stage. His hand came up to squeeze her side as he whispered, "Great job," into her ear. Then he was around her and moving toward the monitor to select his song.

Allie sank gratefully into her seat and Rosie leaned over to give her a one-armed hug. As Kaden scrolled through the list, she couldn't help but admire him anew. He was still in his work clothes, probably hadn't had time to go back to his hotel room, and she couldn't help but notice the way the fabric of his dark slacks hugged his thighs. Wait, were her panties still in his pocket?

As if he could hear her thoughts, he looked up and gave her that damned mischievous smile of his.

There was no way he could have known she was thinking about her panties in his pocket or how those panties had happened to get into his pocket. Could he?

Before she could further panic on that possibility, he selected something on the screen and took the mic. He stepped to the middle of the stage, took a deep breath, and bowed his head. For a moment, the only sound in the room was the dim thump of music from the other sides of the walls.

"All the single ladies!"

The air in Allie's lungs whooshed out in a startled laugh.

"Yes, Beyoncé!" Rosie yelled as she clapped.

Kaden's voice was loud, confident, and completely off-key. It was perfect. Then it got better.

When the chorus came around again, Kaden started to dance, microphone in hand.

The girls lost it, cheering and catcalling as he pranced and dipped and swung his ass around the stage. His dancing was only mildly better than his singing, but he did it with such a wholehearted confidence that Allie couldn't help but kind of love him for it.

"Seriously, dude?" Dean's voice cut through the music. Cass tried to shush him, but he cupped his hands around his mouth and shouted, "Gay!"

"That's fucking *it*." Cass stood up and grabbed Dean by the collar of his shirt, hauling him to his feet despite the fact that he had a good four inches on her. Her eyes blazed with fury. If looks could kill, Dean would already have been bleeding out on the floor.

The song kept going, but Kaden had stopped and was watching the confrontation warily.

"What? It's a joke." Dean shrugged his shoulders, a look of faux innocence on his face.

"No. It wasn't." Cass's manicured finger poked him squarely in the chest. "And we are done. You need to leave."

"Hold up—"

"No. Get lost. And lose my number while you're at it."

For a moment, he just stared at her before anger

bloomed on his face. His eyebrows drew together like small thunderclouds.

Allie glanced at Kaden, who had gone on high alert, like he was preparing to jump in if needed.

Thankfully, it wasn't.

"Fuckin' fine!" Dean finally said as he turned and stormed out of the room, slamming the door as hard as he could on the way out.

Everyone let out a relieved breath. Cass's shoulders slumped as Allie got up to put an arm around her friend.

"You ok?"

Cass scrubbed her hands over her face before letting out a strangled little giggle. "I'm so sorry."

"It's ok, Cass. Really," Grace said as she hugged Cass from the other side and Rosie came up to wrap her arms around all three of them. Or at least what parts she could reach.

"We'd been out on three dates before this and he seemed fine. Nice, even. But…now that I think about it, he didn't drink on any of the dates. And he certainly didn't mention that he was secretly a raging homophobe."

"Better to find out sooner than later," Rosie said, her voice muffled.

Cass patted all the arms she could reach. "I'm really sorry for ruining karaoke night."

"Nonsense, you've ruined nothing." Grace disentangled herself and started pulling people toward the stage, where Kaden stood, looking a little lost. "Group song time. Let's go!"

"'Kiss the Girl'!?" Rosie asked excitedly.

"What else?" came Grace's reply from where she was scrolling through the song list.

The rest of them, including Kaden, crowded in front

of the monitor. Cass still seemed to have a weight on her shoulders, but at least a small smile played on her lips.

Kaden slipped an arm around Allie's shoulders and she leaned in to whisper, "Don't think you've gotten out of that one. I expect you to do the full song and dance before the night is over."

"I look forward to it." His grin was big and infectious.

The song started and soon Dean was just a bad memory as everyone belted out about not being shy. Just kiss the girl. As always, Allie's favorite part was when Rosie would imitate the seagull's warbling cry of "WAAAA. Waaaa. WAAA." It even had Kaden shaking with laughter.

As she swayed with him, singing with her best friends and her best friend from high school, Allie thought maybe inviting Kaden hadn't been such a terrible idea after all.

The rideshare pulled up in front of Allie's building.

"You know your hotel is on the opposite end of town, right?" Allie said.

"Yeah, I know, but this way I got to spend a little more time with you. Besides, the company will pick up the bill. They dragged me up here, after all."

"I'm glad they did."

The back seat of the car was dim, but she could still see Kaden's smile through the shadows. "Me, too."

A weird little flutter of nerves settled into Allie's stomach. "Well, good night."

She opened her door and stepped out of the car. Why was she so awkward?

"Hold up!"

Allie stopped on the sidewalk as Kaden got out of the

car and came around to stand in front of her.

"Have dinner with me tomorrow? Same rules apply. I just want to spend more time with you."

There was such a sweet hopefulness about him that Allie couldn't help but nod in reply. A broad grin broke out on his face and the sight of it warmed her insides.

"Pick you up at seven?"

"Sounds great."

Kaden leaned in and pressed a soft kiss to the corner of her mouth. Just a brief brush of his lips and then he was gone, back into the waiting car.

As she rode the elevator up to her floor, she couldn't help but think back on the strange, surprising, amazing day. One of her fingers came up to brush the corner of her lips. He had been the perfect gentleman all night, just like he'd promised. So why was there a small rock of disappointment lodged in her stomach?

The elevator doors dinged brightly to signal that they had reached her floor. Allie shook herself and strode off down the hallway. She was being ridiculous. Kaden was only in town for another day or two and when he wasn't a gentleman, things like what happened in her office took place. She unlocked her door and stepped inside her dark apartment. It was late. Later than they usually went on karaoke night, but after the Dean Disaster, everyone had wanted to stay and make up for it.

After locking her door and putting her purse on the side table, Allie headed for her bedroom. Seeing Kaden again had gotten her head all twisted around. More than likely, it was just because she'd been single for so long. That had to be it. A good session with her vibrator and sleep would fix her right up and she'd be able to handle a platonic friend dinner tomorrow like a champ. At least, she hoped that would be the case.

FOUR

Allie turned this way and that in front of her mirrored closet door. Her hands smoothed up and down the sides of her red dress, where it hugged her curves before flaring out and ending in a ruffled hem.

"Stop fussing. You look gorgeous." The words came from the dresser where she'd propped her phone so Cass could supervise her getting ready via video call. Cass's long dirty blonde hair was pulled up into a messy ponytail and there were bags under her eyes.

When the call had connected, Allie had tried to get Cass to talk about how she was doing, but the other woman had waved her off. Instead, she insisted on helping Allie pick out an outfit for her dinner. When Cass was in this kind of mood, it was best to not pry. She'd open up when she was ready.

"You sure it's not too much?"

"As Rosie says, 'There's literally no such thing as 'too much' when it comes to fashion.'"

"Says the woman who regularly wears sequined roller

derby shorts to sing karaoke," Allie muttered as she viewed herself from the side one more time. "Maybe I should go with the black one."

"Woman, stop! Please. The black one is boring as hell. Besides, didn't you say he was taking you to that fancy schmancy steak place downtown?" She waited until Allie turned and nodded at her before continuing, "So you should definitely go with this one. Besides, it makes your boobs look huge." Cass's grin was wide and smug.

"Why did I call you instead of Grace or Rosie again?"

"Because Grace is having dinner with her family and Rosie's working the evening shift at the bookstore. But don't worry, I just screenshotted you and sent it to our group text."

Allie let out a groan even as her phone pinged to let her know she had new messages.

"You love me," Cass teased. "Especially because he should be picking you up any minute and now you don't have enough time to get into that funeral dress of yours."

"What?!" Allie snatched up her phone, horrified to realize it was indeed almost seven.

"You're welcome. Love ya, girl. You're going to have a great time. Oh, and find out if Kaden has any hot, single friends." Cass waggled her eyebrows. It was typical Cass, but under her humor was a thread of sadness.

Allie forced out a laugh. "Love ya too, you menace."

She ended the video call and swiped over to her group chat. Despite working, Rosie had already replied to the screenshot of Allie standing in front of her mirror and Grace had hearted the image.

ROSIE:

Looking hot. A+ boobage going on

CASS:

Ha! Told you!

GRACE:

Have fun tonight.

Try the crab cakes for me. I hear they're amazing.

Allie had just sent back a kissy face emoji when a message from Kaden popped up, letting her know he was downstairs. She sent him a quick reply, slipped on her black heels and her light going-out coat. Living in Seattle, she had to have multiple coats with different thicknesses and purposes. The days might still be warm, but the nights got chilly. With one last look at herself in the mirror, she had to admit they'd been right. The sweetheart neckline combined with her best bra did make her tits look amazing.

A live band played slow jazz as Kaden held out her chair at the small table the well-dressed hostess had shown them to. She sat and let him push her forward.

"Thank you."

"My pleasure," he said, taking his own seat and looking around. A series of small tables ringed a small dance floor in front of the stage, where a four-piece band played. Everything was polished wood and dark velvet with brass accents. The lights from the chandeliers overhead were dim and intimate. A long bar with smoked glass shelves ran along one side of the room.

"I hope you don't mind me picking this place. When I saw the menu, I might have drooled a little."

"You drooling over steak? And here I thought after all these years, you'd finally give up your meat-eating ways."

He gave her a smirk. "I'm pretty sure I disproved that in your office yesterday."

A blush heated Allie's cheeks and she ducked behind her menu. A chuckle floated to her from the other side of the table. The menu served double duty of hiding her blush and acting as a barrier so she couldn't stare at him like a lovesick puppy. He'd looked good in his business clothes, but today, in his light gray cashmere sweater, he was devastatingly good looking.

Kaden used one finger to push down the top of her menu.

"Wine?" he asked with a smirk.

"Yes, please."

When the server showed up dressed in a crisp white button-down with a slim black tie, Kaden ordered a bottle of red wine that had a mouthwatering description and a jaw-dropping price point. They ordered and then made small talk until the server brought the bottle of wine.

Once the wine was poured, Kaden lifted his glass. "To old friends?"

"To old friends." Allie gently clinked her glass against his before taking a sip. The wine slipped over her tongue, tasting of blackberries and coffee and something woodsy she couldn't quite put a name to.

"How is it?"

Allie couldn't help but lick her lips. "Delicious."

Kaden grinned back at her. "I've been meaning to tell you how impressed I was with the presentation yesterday."

"Oh, well, thank you. It was a team effort."

"I'm sure it was, but how many times did you personally go over that deck?" Kaden leaned on the table, skewering her with a grin.

"Many," Allie mumbled around her wineglass.

"Uh-huh. It was smart and well put together. The recommendation to change our company name was my favorite part."

"What? You don't like working for a company called 'Blooper?'"

Kaden gave a dramatic shudder. "No. As you might have guessed by the way he defended the name, our head of marketing is pretty set on it. Thinks it makes us appeal to a younger crowd."

"You're selling a product to analyze and visualize large amounts of data in real time for non-tech people. I don't think the 'younger crowd' is your target audience."

"And this is exactly why we hired you."

"Because you're smart." Allie took another sip of her wine. It really was delicious. "I mean, you're the CTO of an up-and-coming startup; of course you're smart. Which reminds me, why isn't your name on the website with the other executives?"

"That's easy. I asked them not to."

"Would have thought you'd gotten more comfortable being online given your career choice."

"Actually, my career choice has only made me more paranoid about what data I share online. The horror stories I could tell you. I'm about this close to replacing my smart phone with a flip phone." He laughed at the expression on Allie's face. "Anyway, how are your parents? What culinary adventures has your dad gotten up to lately?"

"He's currently driving my mother nuts by trying to make every meal in the waffle maker. I'm a bit worried she's going to take a hammer to it one of these days."

"Wait. *Every* meal?"

"Yup. Dad finding foodie Instagram and TikTok has been the bane of my mother's existence."

He let out a laugh that warmed Allie as much as the wine.

"Dungeons crab cakes with heirloom apple slaw with a citrus vinaigrette," the server said, sliding the plate into the middle of the table. "Please enjoy."

Kaden put a forkful of crab cake into his mouth and let out a low sound of appreciation that Allie could feel in the pit of her stomach. Allie made a mental note to text Grace and thank her for the recommendation. As they ate tender, perfectly seasoned crab cakes, they swapped stories about the various adventures they've had over the years and what each of their families had been up to.

Their entrees arrived. As Kaden dug into a beautiful medium-rare steak with mashed potatoes and sautéed vegetables, Allie tried the first bite of her pasta with seared scallops.

"This is amazing."

"Yeah, it is." The look in Kaden's eyes made Allie's insides melt.

His smile shifted into his signature grin as he leaned over the table and speared one of the scallops with his fork.

"Hey!"

"Oh, man. Those are delicious," Kaden said around his mouthful of scallop.

"If I'd know you were still a food stealer, I would have ordered more." Her tone was pouty, but she couldn't help the grin that stretched across her face.

"Some things never change."

"That's for sure." When Kaden went to grab another forkful, she pushed her plate toward him. "Make sure you get some of the pasta. They make the noodles in house."

The conversation shifted to books and movies. Kaden still had a love of terrible sci-fi films—the kind with more fake blood and giant monsters than actual salient plot points.

Those movies had terrified Allie when she was younger, but she'd still watched them with him anyway. She'd tried a couple times as an adult, and while she was no longer scared, it just wasn't the same. There was something missing—a Kaden-sized something she could bury her face into during the jump scares.

Allie was contemplating whether she had enough room for her last bite of creamy noodles (the scallops were long gone) when the bandleader called out, "Gentlefolk, we have a special treat for you tonight. Please welcome to the stage, Miss LaRoux!"

A gorgeous Black woman walked on stage, dressed in a long sequined dress that caught the light like stars. Brilliant pink flowers adorned her hair and matched the color of her lipstick.

"Good evening, everyone. I hope you're all enjoying your dinner. Sure smells good from here." The singer took a mic from one of the stands. "We're going to start off with a bit of a classic. If the music moves you, don't hesitate to come up and dance. Hit it, boys."

The band started a bluesy rendition of "Fly Me to the Moon." Miss LaRoux's voice was smoky and complex. It resonated in Allie's chest, coaxing her soul to soar along with the notes. Across the way, an adorable older couple got up from their table and headed to the dance floor. Allie looked at Kaden and found him with that mischievous grin she knew so well.

"Ohhhh no."

"Ohhhh yes," he said, getting up and extending his hand to her. "One dance, Allie. Please."

With an exaggerated sigh, she put her napkin beside her plate and allowed him to pull her to her feet. When they got to the dance floor, he spun her expertly into his arms and Allie's breath caught in her throat. One of his hands pressed into the small of her back, guiding her in a slow sway to the beat of the music. Underneath the music, she could hear him humming along, terribly off-key.

She smiled to herself. At least he was consistent with his lack of musical ability. It was comforting.

The feel of him warm and solid under her hands was also comforting. Familiar, but not. He spun her out into a twirl and brought her back in, and she let out a laugh. At the sound, his hand flexed on her back and for a moment she thought he would pull her in closer, but then he relaxed, maintaining the small gap between their bodies. Allie knew he was just keeping his word about keeping his hands to himself. She couldn't help but feel a ping of disappointment. He spun her out again, obliterating all thoughts except the music and the feel of their bodies moving together on the dance floor.

After three songs, Allie was warm and a little breathless.

"Do you want to head back to the table and order dessert?" Kaden leaned down to whisper in her ear even as the band started into a new song. "I noticed they have carrot cake with cream cheese frosting."

The mention of frosting brought another thought to mind. Maybe it was the surrealism of the whole thing—seeing Kaden so unexpectedly after so long, then the whole thing in her office—or perhaps it was the excellent wine, but Allie was feeling bold. Bolder than she'd felt in so long.

"Why don't we head back to my place…for dessert?"

Kaden's shoulders stiffened under her hands for just the briefest moment, before he chuckled. "That sounds perfect. Let me get the check and we'll get out of here."

FIVE

They made it through her door, and Allie had just enough time to get nervous about showing Kaden her apartment when he pressed her against the wall of her entryway. His kiss took her breath and every thought from her head. All she could do was kiss him back, marveling at the way their lips fit together. When his tongue swept into her mouth, she melted against him.

He tasted like wine and Allie couldn't get enough. Her hands came up to tangle in his hair. It still had that faintly coarse texture to it, just as it had in high school, and felt both soft and just a little rough.

Strong hands smoothed up her sides and his thumbs smoothed along the bottom of her breasts. Even through the fabric of her dress, it made her arch and squirm, wanting more. His thumbs found her already stiff nipples and began teasing them in sweeping motions as his mouth left hers and kissed along her jaw and then down the column of her throat. Her breath hitched and pushed up on her toes to allow him more access.

He licked and kissed and sucked his way down from her

collarbone to the edge of her dress. A small gasp fell from her mouth as his thumbs stopped their teasing and pulled the collar of her dress down, exposing the lace of her bra. Kaden let out a low hum of pleasure as his mouth skated over the lace.

Her hands were still tangled in his hair and she wasn't sure if she was trying to pull him closer or push him away as he sucked and licked, each pull of his mouth sending little bolts of pleasure down her spine and just making her ache more for him.

The hard press of his jean-clad cock on her upper thigh made her hips roll. He let out a low moan, his mouth still around her nipple, the lace of her bra soaked from his attentions.

"Wait," she said, the word a low, breathless rasp.

Immediately, Kaden straightened and asked, "Everything all right?"

She smiled even as she took a couple of breaths to clear her head. Instead of answering him, she took his hand and started pulling him toward her bedroom. He'd made her see stars earlier in her office. Now it was her turn.

Once inside the door, Kaden gave the room a quick once-over. She'd painted it a pale lavender color. Just because Seattle spent nine months of the year shrouded in gray, it didn't mean she wanted to live in a colorless world.

His eyes caught on the painting hanging over her dresser. She'd picked it up on a visit to Hawaii and spent more money on it than she'd have liked, but something about the tropical flowers in their riot of rainbow colors had called to her.

There would be time for him to explore her space later. Allie put her hands on Kaden's chest and pushed him down on the edge of her bed.

He let out a startled chuckle. "Yes? Can I help you?"

"Nope." She pulled the zipper down the back of her dress and let the material pool at her feet before stepping out of it.

"You sure?" Kaden pulled the sweater over his head and tossed it away.

Her hands traced down the planes of his chest, her fingers trailing through the light smattering of hair that covered it. She followed her hands down until she was on her knees in front of him.

"Positive. If this is ok with you, of course?"

"Oh, yeah. No, this is totally fine." Kaden kicked off his shoes before leaning back on his hands and grinning down at her. "Please, continue."

The leather of his belt was smooth in her hands as she unbuckled it before undoing the button and zipper on his dark jeans. Gripping them and the band of the navy boxer-briefs, she waited until he lifted his hips and she could pull them down his thighs. Her hands faltered as his dick sprung free. It was long and perfectly curved and she could only imagine how delicious it would feel deep in her. Filling her. Stroking every inch of her.

"Enjoying the view?"

Allie jumped, heat rising in her cheeks before she stuck her tongue out at him. Kaden's answering laughter was cut off when she wrapped her lips around the head of his cock.

"Fuccccckkkk me."

"That's the plan," Allie mumbled around him as she worked his pants off and tossed them in the same general direction he'd sent his sweater.

The taste of him was soft and salty on her tongue as she worked her way up and down his shaft slowly, taking her time to explore every inch of him. Her hands splayed on the tops of his thighs, feeling the muscles twitch under her hands.

Slowly she started increased her rhythm, pausing to lick and suck at the crown before starting another descent to take him as far as she could into her mouth. It wasn't as far as she'd have liked—her gag reflex had always been a bit too enthusiastic—but she made up for it by curling her hand around his base and stroking him in time with her mouth.

"Goddamn, Allie. Look at you." His words were low and rough and full of appreciation. "I can't tell you how many times I've thought about having my cock in your mouth over the years, but fuck, it can't compare to the real thing."

The words sent little flutters down Allie's spine. She couldn't help but glance sideways at the mirrored door of her closet. The sight nearly took her breath away: Kaden in all his naked glory on her bed, his whole being focused on her mouth. Her kneeling in front of him with her lips halfway down his cock. It made her pussy ache and she rubbed her thighs together, desperately seeking a little friction, something to take the edge off.

But this wasn't about her, she reminded herself as she started working him again. Even as she increased her pace, her hand working in tandem with her mouth, she couldn't help sneaking peeks at the mirror, relishing the way his forearms tensed as he gripped the comforter or the way the muscles in his stomach bunched and tensed. The way his cock looked, slick and shiny, as she worked her mouth up and down.

Little moans and pants were falling from his mouth and she couldn't help the swell of pride that rose in her, knowing she had caused them.

Then a hand was in her hair, gripping tight, holding

her in place. Kaden pulled her off his length and she looked up at him, her eyebrows furrowed in question.

"Everything ok?"

One hand stayed in her hair as the other traced along her jaw. His thumb came up to brush her bottom lip. "More than ok. Fucking phenomenal, but as amazing as your mouth feels, I'd rather be in something else." He leaned forward and kissed her softly. The hand in her hair tugged just enough to force her head back. His other hand slid down between her legs and ghosted along her soaked panties. "Can I fuck you, Allie?"

"Yes. Yes, please."

His finger slipped past the edge of her panties and plunged inside her. She let out a small cry that was quickly swallowed by Kaden's mouth. He kissed her hard, his tongue stroking into her mouth at the same time as his finger pushed into and out of her pussy.

A second finger slipped inside her and she spread her knees wider, giving him better access. His thumb found her clit, pressing little circles that made her blood sing in her veins.

The hand in her hair kept her in place even as his other hand drove her higher and higher until warmth burst from her stomach and her body tensed. Pleasure washed through her.

His hands and kisses slowed. "Just beautiful," he said, before giving her another lingering kiss. "I assume condoms are in the top drawer of your nightstand?"

"Uh… what? Yes."

Condoms. Yes. They needed one of those. She was glad he was able to think, because her ability to do so had abandoned her about the same time he'd wrapped her hair around his fingers.

He left her kneeling on the floor and went over to the nightstand and began rummaging around.

"Oh, could you grab the lube too, please?"

"Of course. Wait." He held up her pink plastic egg. "This can't be your only vibrator. Is it?"

"Yeah? Why?"

"This thing uses batteries! This was, like, the height of orgasm tech thirty years ago." He held the little remote that was attached to the egg by a string with a look of horrified fascination on his face.

Allie crossed her arms over her breasts. "So? I like it, ok?"

He gave her a hard look. "Do you like it because you enjoy the feeling it gives you or because it's safe and nonthreatening?"

"I don't know what you mean." Damn that man for knowing her too well, even after all these years.

It wasn't that she didn't masturbate or was a virgin, but her mom's lessons about being "a proper young lady" hadn't only applied to how to act in public. Her sex education had been sterile, practical, and medically inclined. After the incident at her cousin's wedding, there had been a lot of guilt and a lot of soul-searching about whether she was a deviant or twisted not just for allowing it to happen, but for enjoying it so thoroughly.

She'd gotten over that part but still hadn't felt the need to explore the full spectrum of sex toys.

"It gets me off just fine."

He let out a chuckle as he grabbed a condom and lube and stalked back to her, the pink egg still held in his other hand. He held out the foil packet. "Please put this on me, Allie."

Despite the fact that she was still a little miffed at him, she couldn't help but respond to the command in his voice.

To the promise of him fucking her with that ludicrously perfect cock of his. She took the condom. After opening the packet, she rolled it down his length, taking her time to smooth it out and make sure nothing pinched.

Then she grabbed the bottle of lube he held out to her and squeezed a generous amount into her palm. She looked up at his face as she smoothed the cool liquid down his cock. His eyes closed as a low hiss slipped from his lips. The sound flowed straight to her core and made her thighs clench. A few more strokes and her hand slid easily up and down his shaft.

She stood, unhooked her bra, and slid it off. Kaden's eyes were hungry as he watched her shimmy out of her panties and turned toward the bed.

"Where are you going?" he asked, snagging her wrist.

"Um, the bed?"

He pulled her back so her back was to his chest. Soft lips offset by the scrape of his beard ghosted along her shoulder. "Eyes up, sweetheart."

Allie's gaze rose to the mirror and her breath caught. They were a hell of a sight together. He was looking at her over her shoulder, his eyes heavy-lidded and intense. One hand rose to cup her breast and she arched into it. His fingers gently pinched her nipple. She couldn't help but roll her hips, pressing her ass into him, feeling the length of his cock pressed between them.

His hand skimmed down her stomach and came to rest over her shaved pussy. She shifted her stance, widening her legs to give him more room. Her breathing was short and fast, her eyes glued to where his long fingers spread her open, exposing her wet lips to the mirror.

"Look at you, so responsive and needy. So fucking perfect." He kissed the side of her neck, nibbling up to her ear. His words were soft and rough and sent little shivers of pleasure and need down her spine. "If I ever do anything you don't like, just say the word 'stop.' Do you understand?"

"Yes."

"Good. Now spread yourself open for me. I want you to watch as that pretty pussy of yours takes every inch of me."

Her breath hitched and her hands shook as she hurried to obey him. The Kaden Allie remembered didn't talk like this, wasn't crude. Not even the Kaden at dinner talked like this, but damn, listening to his dirty mouth only made her even more wet and needy.

The warmth of him retreated as he gripped his cock and lined it up at her entrance. Her eyes were riveted to where the head of his cock slipped between her open folds.

But that was as far as he went.

Allie shifted and squirmed, trying to get him inside her to no avail.

"Kaden...please." The word was so high and needy, Allie almost didn't recognize her own voice.

A low chuckle came from behind her, but thankfully he stopped teasing her and slid just the head of him into her. The breath caught in her throat. Her entire body focused on the delicious stretch of him.

Almost painfully slowly, he pushed into her. Her head fell back against his shoulder, but she couldn't help but keep her eyes glued to the mirror, watching where her hands held herself open. Where his cock slowly parted her, disappearing within her inch by inch. It was the hottest thing she'd ever done in her life. Hell, it was the hottest thing she'd ever even fantasized about before.

When he was fully seated inside her, Allie's gaze flicked up to where Kaden's chin rested on her shoulder. His own gaze was riveted to where they were joined in the mirror.

He let out a long, ragged breath. "Jesus, woman. You might kill me."

"You'll kill me first if you don't start moving soon." She clenched around him and was rewarded with a twitch of his cock deep inside her.

"So impatient." He pressed a kiss to her shoulder and pulled out of her before fucking back in slowly.

Her breathing increased as he steadily built up his rhythm. Each slide of his cock stretched her walls, setting every one of her nerves alight. And she got to watch every second of it.

"Hold this for me."

"Wha—?" Allie pulled her attention away from the mirror long enough to take the egg end of her vibrator from him. "Oh!"

The remote was still in his hands and he flicked the wheel, causing the egg to vibrate in her hand.

"Use that on yourself." Teeth dragged along the column of her throat, followed by open-mouthed kisses to soothe the scrape. "I want to watch you, feel you, break apart around me."

A desperate little whimper fell from her mouth as she pressed the smooth plastic of the egg to her aching clit.

"Oh, God." Tremors started at the tops of her thighs as the egg sent waves of pleasure spiraling out from her core.

Kaden snapped his hips, driving himself a little harder, a little deeper into her.

"Yes. Please. Just like that."

Heat built in her stomach, radiating out to her limbs. Her legs shook as she kept the egg pressed against her clit, her fingers slick with lube and her own wetness. Pressure built in her chest, her breathing harsh and ragged. Despite herself, her closed her eyes, everything focused on the feeling of him fucking her and the egg's persistent buzz.

"None of that, sweetheart. Keep those eyes open." His free hand came up to gently wrap around her neck, forcing her head up. She blinked her eyes open, her whole body wound tight, her breath catching and holding in her chest.

A ragged cry spilled from her mouth as her whole body tensed. The orgasm washed through her as every muscle clenched and then released, spilling bright pleasure from her head to her toes.

The still buzzing vibrator was almost too much and she moved her hand away, but Kaden caught her wrist.

"I think you've got one more in you." He cranked up the strength on the vibrator until it sounded like the buzz of an angry hornet and forced her hand back down to her clit.

"Holy fuck!"

Allie tried to squirm away from the overwhelming sensation, but Kaden still had one hand on her throat, not squeezing, just holding her in place. There was nowhere for her to go, nothing she could do but endure as the vibrator shoved her back toward an orgasm. She could have told him to stop and he would have done so the second she said it, but why in the world would she want to?

Kaden's thrusts turned short and driving, keeping her completely filled. Her first orgasm had been amazing, but it was nothing compared to the one building in her core. This was a tidal wave, a hurricane.

"That's it, sweetheart. Come for me."

Kaden's words, harsh and broken with his own need, undid her. She crashed headfirst into her orgasm. A desperate cry ripped from her and despite her best efforts, her eyes closed as her pussy clenched over and over on Kaden's cock, trying to pull him even deeper.

As the aftershocks swept through her, the motion of his hips sped up, losing their precise rhythm. She was just able to drag her eyes open in time to watch his beautiful face tip back toward the ceiling as he buried himself deep within her, his arms holding her tight to his chest as his own pleasure cascaded inside her.

The two of them stood for a long moment, each trying to catch their breath. Then Allie's trembling legs lost their fight with gravity and would have sent her crashing to the carpet had Kaden not shifted his grip to her waist.

"Thanks." The word was as breathy and fragile as she felt.

"Let's get you into bed." He turned off the still buzzing vibrator before helping her over to the bed and under the covers. Leaning down, he pressed a kiss to her lips before saying, "Be right back."

Allie floated in her body, every nerve fuzzy and light, as Kaden went into the bathroom to dispose of the condom and clean up. When he slid back into her bed after turning off the light, she turned on her side and he snuggled against her back. A warm hand curled around her side and pressed flat against her stomach. The heavy warmth of him was soothing, grounding. He heaved a sigh and his breath tickled the back of her neck before his arm tightened around her in a gentle squeeze.

"I...don't really have words for how good that was. Or for how long I've wanted to do that." Kaden's words were soft and warmed Allie from the inside.

Allie entwined her fingers with Kaden's. "Me too." It was a truth made easy to share because of the languid feeling in her limbs, the gentle ache of her expertly used pussy, and Kaden's own sweet admission.

Head quieter than it had been in years, Allie fell asleep to the comforting sound of Kaden's deep, even breathing.

SIX

In the morning, Allie woke with a start. The other side of the bed was rumpled, but completely empty. She relaxed back onto her pillow with a sigh and wrestled with the warring feelings of hurt and relief. On one hand, it would serve her right for him to sneak away in the night without a goodbye, especially after she'd ghosted him. On the other, her heart ached. She didn't want to examine that feeling too closely. This was for the best.

It wasn't like there could be anything else between them. A pleasurable closure. That was all it was.

Then the door to her bathroom opened and Kaden walked in, his damp, dark hair sticking up in all directions. A towel was slung low over his hips and desire punched Allie in the gut. How was it that this man could get her that revved up just by walking into a room? No one had ever had that effect on her. No one had ever made her lose her mind and sanity so much that she did risky, terrible things like letting him go down on her in the office, with her coworkers just outside the door.

"Hey, sweetheart," Kaden said as he started gathering

up his clothes. "I'm sorry for waking you, but I've got to get back to my hotel. Flight is in a couple of hours." He paused as he got his boxer-briefs and jeans back on. "I was thinking I could come back up next weekend? Maybe we could catch a Seahawks game." When Allie didn't reply, he looked up at her and paused. "Allie, no. Don't panic on me, sweetheart."

He moved over to the bed and reached a hand out to her, but she cringed away before he could touch her. His hand dropped back to his side.

Allie's heart sank at the look of hurt on his face. But what else could she do? This wasn't realistic. She sat up, carefully gathering the sheet over her breasts.

"Last night was…fun, Kaden. But you live in LA and I live in Seattle—"

"It's only a three-hour plane ride away. That's not a good enough excuse." He crossed his arms over his bare chest and Allie couldn't help but wish he'd gotten fully dressed before they had this conversation. He was distracting and that was a big part of the problem. It had only been two days since he'd waltzed back into her life and look at the chaos he'd already caused.

"It's been years. We don't know each other at all."

Kaden raked one hand through his hair and let out a harsh bark of a laugh. "More bullshit, Allie. Yeah, we haven't seen each other in years, but we know each other. It might not be easy, but we could work. We could be really good together. I'm not asking you to elope in Vegas. Just give us a chance, please. Give me a chance."

"I…can't." It wouldn't work. Long distance never worked out. All she was doing was setting herself up to have her heart ripped out later down the line. If she was this head over heels for him after two days together, there was no way she would survive a relationship with him. Not with her sanity and dignity intact.

"Great. Just perfect." He snatched up his sweater and jerked it on with quick, angry movements. After he picked up his socks and shoes, he turned back to where Allie sat in a miserable ball on the bed. "I'm not going to chase you this time. This is it, Allie. I deserve someone who will fight just as hard to be with me as I would to be with them. My bad for thinking maybe you'd grown some backbone over the years. You're still running away from the good things in your life because they fucking scare you. Like a coward."

The words were knives that stabbed into Allie's chest, stealing her breath. She wanted to refute them. To yell and scream and throw those words back at Kaden so they would slice his chest open to match hers. But she was frozen. Locked inside her body, awash in pain, and unable to make a peep.

He looked like he was going to say something else, but only closed his mouth with a hard click. Shaking his head, he turned and walked out of her bedroom barefoot, his shoes still held in his hand. The sound of her front door closing seemed to reverberate throughout her apartment and deep within her bones.

"Kaden..." The word was soft. A whisper of sound. Just a breath as it passed her lips.

And with it came more pain, as though her heart, which had been missing for these last twelve years, had finally been returned, only to be ripped from her chest once more.

Allie slumped down in her bed, curled around herself, and sobbed.

~

Allie spent Sunday on the couch watching bad movies and ignoring her group text, which was mostly the girls asking about how the night had gone. She'd tell them, eventually. She just wasn't ready yet. They loved her and wouldn't let her wallow, but wallowing was all she wanted right now.

Monday morning came against her wishes. Work was supposed to help, but somehow it was worse than just being a lump on the couch. To do her job, she needed to be chipper, upbeat. She couldn't allow the fact that her heart felt like it had been freeze-dried and reconstituted with battery acid and tears to show.

Tuesday was just as miserable as Monday. In fact, the entire week was one long slog. It took every ounce of her strength to make it through each day of answering emails, attending meetings, and putting together marketing plans and presentations. Each night she came home, shoved something in her mouth for dinner, drank wine in the bath-tub, and passed out on the couch.

She kept telling herself she'd made the right choice. A future with Kaden had been a fantasy. Something that would never work out. She'd just stopped things before she could get attached, before she could really get hurt.

So why was it that on Friday, instead of being excited about the weekend, all she could think about was her date a week ago and how it had felt to dance with Kaden to slow, seductive jazz?

Her footsteps were slow and heavy as she dragged herself into the lobby of her building. A vibration from her purse let her know she had a text message. Probably from Grace or Rosie, since Cass was on another first date. They were worried about Allie and probably wanted to convince her to get dinner and watch a movie or something, but she just didn't have the energy for it. She stood for a moment, looking between the elevator and the door to the mailroom. She hadn't checked her mailbox all week and the junk was probably overflowing.

Heaving a sigh, she plastered on a smile and pushed open the door.

Mr. González greeted her from behind his counter. "Happy Friday, Ms. Allie! Exciting weekend plans?"

"Happy Friday, Mr. G." Allie usually loved to stop and chat with the elderly Mexican gentleman who managed the building mailroom better than the United States Postal Service. Today she went straight to her box in the middle of the rows of metal doors that lined the walls and unlocked it. A small cascade of flyers, bills, and credit card applications tumbled out and Allie hurried to stuff them into her bag before they could sail to the tiled floor. While stuffing the unruly papers into her purse, she tried to hurry out of the room.

"Wait, Ms. Allie. You have a package."

Allie stopped with her hand on the door. "What?"

Mr. G gave her a small smile and pushed a shoebox-sized cardboard package across the top of the counter.

"Huh. I don't remember ordering anything. Thanks, Mr. G." Allie juggled her purse and laptop bag so she could grab the box under one arm. It was plain brown box with a P.O. return address from somewhere in Idaho.

"Maybe it's a gift," Mr. G said with a shrug. "Have a great weekend, Ms. Allie."

"Maybe. Have a good one."

Absently she pushed her way through the door and back towards the elevator. All the way up to her floor, she kept racking her brains, trying to figure out what could possibly be in the box. Yes, she'd been having more wine at night than usual, but she wasn't a drunk shopper. Drunk crier, sure. Maybe Mr. G was right and her dad had sent her a present. But his presents tended to be in the form of vacuum-packed homemade baked goods. They were always a bit squashed, but that didn't detract from the flavor. Could he have branched out into sending her kitchen equipment?

After getting into her apartment, she dropped her bags and set the box on her small kitchen table. The little paring knife sliced easily through the tape on the top. When the flaps were pulled back, brown packing paper greeted her. Throwing it to the side, Allie let out a small little "oh" as her heart started beating faster in her chest. She pulled out the packing slip and felt all her blood drain into her feet.

With shaking hands, she dove for her purse, pulled out her phone, and sent out a distress call.

Allie threw open the door and shoved a glass of wine into Cass's hand.

"Um, hello to you, too." Case took a sip as she entered Allie's apartment and closed the door behind her. "I could get used to this kind of welcome. Especially since your text got me out of what was shaping up to be the most boring date I've ever had in my life. Heya, Grace and Rosie. Has Allie told you why she called this emergency meeting?"

The two waved from their chairs around Allie's table.

Grace shook her head. Today she was wearing large, round tortoiseshell glasses. "Nope. Refused to say anything until you got here. She's a mess, though."

"She's standing right here," Allie said, crossing her arms over her favorite faded pink sweatshirt.

Cass looped her arm around Allie's shoulders and gave her a squeeze. "Sorry, girlie. What happened?"

"That happened." Allie dropped into a chair with a huff and pointed to the open package on her table.

Her three friends shared a look as Cass took a seat and Grace pulled the box over. Grace's eyebrows shot up into her bangs as she looked back to where Allie slumped in her chair.

"It's a vibrator…"

"What?! Let me see!" Cass reached in and pulled out a slick white and purple box. "Yup. It's a vibrator. I mean, it's a very nice, high-end vibrator, but it's still just a vibrator. You're a big girl with a good job. You can buy yourself as many toys as you want. I got to tell you, I'm really confused here."

"Oh, I've heard that one is amazing. Been meaning to buy one myself," Rosie said, leaning over to peer at the packaging.

Allie pulled a folded piece of paper from her pocket and slid it across the table. It was a gift receipt. She braced her elbows on the table, covering her face with her hands as Grace picked it up and read:

Just a little something to keep you company until the next time. Hope it's not too intimidating. :P
-Kaden

"Wait, Kaden?" Rosie said, snatching the paper and rereading it like it contained clues to a lost treasure or, in Rosie's case, to mint-condition first editions of her favorite books. "Kaden, the old friend who you brought to karaoke and then had dinner with last week?"

"Yes, Rosie. That Kaden." Allie didn't bother to remove her hands from her face, so the words came out muffled.

"You totally banged his brains out after dinner, didn't

you?" Cass asked as she leaned over the table.

Allie let out a reluctant affirmative.

"I still don't see what the issue is," Grace said. "So you slept with the guy and he sent you a gift. Where's the problem?"

Mumble. Mumble. Mumble.

"Girl, sit up," Rosie groused. "We want to help you, but you have to actually tell us what is going on."

With a deep breath, Allie sat up straight. "He wanted to keep seeing each other, and the morning after our night together, I told him I didn't want to do a long-distance relationship."

"Well, that's just creepy then. Want me to fly to wherever he's from and kill him?" Rosie asked.

Allie looked startled. "What? No! It's not creepy."

Cass, Grace, and Rosie shared another look before Cass reached over and took her hand. "Sweetie, you told him to get lost and he sent you a vibrator accompanied by, frankly, a threatening message."

"Oh. I could see how you'd think that." She pulled the gift receipt back to her and pointed to the date/time stamp at the top. "Look, he made the purchase early on Saturday morning. Before we talked. Probably before he got into the shower."

"Huh, yeah. That does change things. Takes it from 'ew, creep' to 'awww, sweet,'" Rosie said, taking a sip of wine. "Though, you'd think he'd cancel the order after you kicked his ass to the curb."

"He must have forgotten." Allie put her head in her hands again. "Ughhhhh. What am I going to do?"

"Return it?" Grace said.

"Use it?" Cass countered.

Allie shot her friend a death glare.

Cass held up her hands in surrender. "I'm just saying.

It's a really nice vibrator. It's even waterproof."

"Super helpful, Cass. Really."

Rosie took Allie's hand. Her face was uncharacteristically serious. "I know you told us you don't want to do a long-distance relationship and that's valid, but are you, maybe, rethinking your decision?"

"Why do you ask?"

She glanced at Cass, who said, "Frankly, you look terrible."

"Gee, thanks."

"Bit harsh, Cass," Grace chided, before reaching over to squeeze Allie's other hand. "But not wholly untrue. When was the last time you had a good night's sleep?"

"Ummmm—"

"I'm guessing it was the same night Kaden slept over. The bags under your eyes are the size of Lake Union." Grace's tone was gently teasing, but there was genuine concern on her face. "You don't lose sleep over men. Ever."

"She's right. You didn't even cry when that dirtbag cheated on you a couple of years ago," Rosie offered.

Allie jerked back, freeing her hands from her friends' well-meaning grips. Her mouth opened, but she snapped it closed and opted to grab the open bottle and poured more wine into her glass, even if she didn't particularly need a refill. "So? We'd only been dating a year and I knew it wasn't going to last."

Rosie fiddled with the stem of her wineglass. "That's kind of the point. You go into relationships *knowing* that they're not going to last. Hell, sometimes it's like you've already got your foot out the door before you even start dating the guy."

"That's exactly what it's like." Cass held out her glass to Rosie, who clinked hers against it.

"You know, I didn't call you over to pick apart the entirety of my sorry love life," Allie said into her wineglass.

Her friends exchanged glances again. Cass's hand snatched Allie's wineglass from her.

"Hey!"

"I'll give it back once you stop hiding behind it and start being honest with us. And yourself. What's the real reason you turned down the man who finger-banged you at a wedding while listening to a man's unholy love of aquatic creatures?" Cass's eyebrows rose as she smirked at a horrified Allie.

"Wait," Grace said, holding up a hand. "Wait. Are you saying that Kaden is 'Magic Finger Man'?"

Allie was starting to regret having told them about the incident at her cousin's wedding. The three of them had been "karaoke drunk" one night, as Rosie liked to call it. They'd been swapping scandalous stories and none of Allie's had been nearly as exciting or risqué as the ones the others were telling, so she'd told the only one she had.

"The man knows all the dance moves to "Single Ladies" and seems like he could talk a nun into a three-some." One of the "karaoke drunk" nights, they'd learned that Grace had a serious soft spot for dirty talk.

"Yes! Kaden is Magic Finger Man." Allie had really been hoping they would never make that connection, but Cass had a sixth sense when it came to all things even remotely kinky. "But that doesn't change anything. Like I told you, long-distance relationships never—"

"She's never getting her wine back," Rosie said to Cass with a sad shake of her head. "Want to split it?"

Allie pulled her hands into the sleeves, her nails picking at the frayed edges of her cuffs. It didn't matter that she was almost thirty-three years old, habits and all that. She took a deep breath. "He makes me…messy."

"What do you mean, messy?" Grace asked.

"There's something about him. I completely lose my head with him and end up doing reckless things."

"The wedding was ages ago" Cass said before sitting up straight when she saw the blush that lit up Allie's cheeks. "Or did something else happen that you haven't told us about yet?"

Hiding her head in her hands, Allie mumbled a reply.

"Wait, did she just say she got eaten out in her office?!" Rosie said, leaning back from the table, her eyes wide.

"I mean, not in those words, but yeah, she did," Cass confirmed, a note of pride in her voice.

Allie dragged her hands down her face.

"Never thought you'd have it in you," Cass said, leaning over to lightly punch Allie on the arm.

Rosie looked at Allie critically for a moment. "What I don't get is how you two went from not talking for years to having him eat you like his birthday cake in the span of a business presentation?"

If it was possible for someone to die of humiliation, Allie was sure she was in mortal danger.

"I might have been…relieving some tension when he came in," Allie admitted, before reaching out her hand. "Can I please have my wine back now?"

"Oh, yeah, no. That's the definition of messy. Here. You've earned it." Grace reached across the table and slid the glass back to Allie.

Allie nodded a thanks before taking a very long sip.

"So your old flame walks in on you petting your kitty in your office and then gets down on his knees and helps you finish the job? I'm really starting to like this guy."

"Good, I'm so glad, Cass. However, you've forgotten that we aren't a thing."

"But you could be." Grace just shrugged when Allie

blinked at her. "It sounds like he wants you to be. Or at least to give it a try. If 'messy' is the problem, just tell him no being messy in public. If he doesn't respect that boundary, then he isn't worth your time."

Allie couldn't help it; her mind went back to how he'd fucked her in front of her mirror. The way he'd made her watch as he'd slid in and out of her. How safe and confident and needy she'd felt with him. He'd said he liked her that way. Could it really be that easy? He had promised to keep his hands to himself at karaoke and dinner and he'd been the perfect gentleman. At least until they'd gotten home.

"The cogs in your brain are starting to smoke," Cass teased. "Lubricate them with more wine. Or at least pass the bottle so I can refill my glass."

Absently, Allie handed the bottle over to her. As Cass refilled glasses, a fresh worry crept up Allie's spine.

"But what do I say? How do I even go about this? Just call him up and go, 'sorry for being a complete coward. Can we try again?'"

"I mean, it might work, but it's also kind of terrible," Rosie said with a wince. "How about we finish this bottle and help you brainstorm?"

A mixture of hope and fear and gratitude had tears pricking at the corners of her eyes. "Thanks. I'm really lucky to have you all."

"Damn right you are. And maybe later tonight you could try this bad boy out. You know, for 'inspiration.'" Cass picked up the box with the vibrator in it and made it dance across the table toward Allie.

"Stop!" Allie laughed and swiped the box from Cass before tossing it back into the plain cardboard box it had arrived in.

Though, it did give her the start of an idea.

SEVEN

Kaden's condo was at the end of a street of new two-story homes with attached garages and no yards. They were all done in various shades of grays and blues. Kaden's was a dark blue that was almost navy in the shadows with white trim. Light illuminated the downstairs windows, letting her know that someone was home.

"Oh, this is the worst idea ever," Allie said in a singsong voice to herself as she brought Kaden's phone number up in her contacts. She was in a rental car parked down the street from his house. "How did I let them talk me into this? Oh yeah, with a whole bottle of red. That's how. Jesus, Allie. Stop talking to yourself and call him."

Before she could chicken out and fly back to Seattle, she pressed the call button. It seemed to ring for eternity, but was probably only four or five times. Just long enough for her to panic about whether he was screening her calls and if so, what the fuck she'd say if he sent her to voicemail.

"Allie?"

The relief from hearing Kaden's voice was immediately tempered by how wary he sounded. It made her heart hurt because she knew it was completely warranted and her own damned fault.

"Um, hi. Is now a good time to talk?"

"Yes, just give me a minute." Muted sounds of a sports announcer narrating a game filtered through the phone, but it got fainter until the sound of a door closing cut it off completely.

"Oh, I'm sorry. If now isn't a good time, I could call back later or tomorrow. Or you could call me."

"Allie." His voice held a hint of exasperated amusement, which was definitely a step up from distant and weary. "It's fine. What do you need?"

"I." Allie took a deep breath. "I want to apologize."

Over the line came a long exhale, but Kaden didn't say anything.

"You were right. I was scared. No one has ever made me feel like you do. You slip through all my defenses and that terrifies me. You know me—even after all this time, you still know me—I don't do reckless things. I don't do things without thinking them through a million times and having at least four backup plans."

Kaden let out a chuckle that made Allie's heart skip in her chest. "True, I was always the one getting you into trouble when we were growing up."

"Yes, and I always got us out of it. But as much as I bitched and moaned, those memories are some of my favorites."

"Mine too."

"Kaden, you're worth being vulnerable for. You're worth getting into a bit of trouble for. I know I screwed up, but I really want to try and make this work. Please."

A sharp intake of breath came across the line and then

nothing. It was silent for so long, Allie actually checked to make sure they were still connected.

"Kaden? Look, if you don't want to or if I lost my chance, that's okay. Really, you—"

"Allie." The sharp command in his voice cut through her panicked rambling and she closed her mouth with a click. "You just surprised me. It's one of the things that I've always loved about you. Yes, I'd like to give this—us—a real try."

It was as if all the bones in Allie's body melted as she slumped in the front seat. A joyous laugh bubbled out of her.

"How about I come up to Seattle next weekend? You can show me around and we can spend some time seeing how this works."

"That sounds great," she said, forcing herself to sit up straighter. "I do have one request, though."

"All right?" Some of the wariness had come back into his voice.

"I'd like to keep the sexy times in the bedroom. Or at the very least, in our homes?"

"Ahh. And here I thought you enjoyed what happened in your office," Kaden said, his voice teasing.

"You know I did. But that's the problem. I liked it too much. But what I didn't like was the anxiety and worry I felt afterwards, wondering if my coworkers heard and were just being nice and ignoring me until we all got called into a big HR 'No Sex on Company Time' meeting with my face on the first slide."

"That…that's not a thing. You know that wouldn't happen, right?"

Allie let out a long breath. "Logically, I know that, but try telling that to my brain."

"So public sex is off the table. I think I can make that sacrifice. What about kissing? Holding hands?"

"Totally on the table. Everything we did after dinner at my place? Enthusiastically on the table. Just behind closed doors."

"Good to know." Kaden sucked in a breath. "That was a very good night. I can't wait to revisit it next weekend."

"Me too. Oh, I wanted to thank you for the present."

"Present? What present?"

"The, um, *intimidating* one."

There was a sound that could only have been Kaden smacking his forehead with the palm of his hand. "Oh God. I'm so sorry. I ordered it before I got into the shower at your place and completely forgot about it. You must have thought I was a total jackass."

"No, no. It's okay. Really. I definitely don't think you're a jackass. Maybe a creep," Allie couldn't help but tease.

"Oh, yeah, a creep is totally better than being a jackass."

Allie giggled. "I'm just teasing. I didn't think it was creepy. In fact, I enjoyed it. Thoroughly."

"Mmm. In that case, I retract my apology."

"Would you like a 'thank you' video?"

"Does it involve you using your present?"

"Maybe."

"Yes. Yes, I would."

"I'm going to send it to you. Call me back after you watch it." Allie hung up before Kaden could respond and quickly sent him the short video.

Instead of just sitting in the unfamiliar car, counting the seconds until he called back, Allie pulled up the video and hit Play. She'd probably watched it at least a dozen times already, not out of vanity necessarily, but because she wanted it to be perfect for him.

It opened with her sitting on the edge of her bed, wearing a white and pink lace teddy. She'd ordered a tripod and ring light just to make the video, and had tidied her bedroom to a degree it hadn't seen since she'd moved in. She'd debated going for a full face of makeup but had settled on only light pink gloss and having her hair in loose waves down her back.

Kaden's gift was held in one hand. It was a pale purple and made of soft silicone. There was a central shaft and an extension that teased your clit when fully inserted. After thanking him profusely for her present, she turned it on, letting it buzz against the lace covering her breasts, slipping it down over her stomach, and then along the inside of her thigh, opening her legs and showing off the matching lace of her thong.

She leaned back on her free hand as she ran the toy over her barely concealed pussy, letting herself shiver and bite her lip with the sensation.

"As fun as my new toy is," she said, her voice a little breathless, "I'd rather you were here to use it on me. But I'll just have to make do."

Sitting up, she toyed with the lace edge of her panties. One painted fingernail hooked the edge and moved it aside. The long, thick shaft of the vibrator lined up, ready to plunge into her wet pussy, when the video ended on a black screen with the words "call for more" in big block letters.

The video had barely finished on Allie's phone before she got a notification for an incoming call. She hit the Accept button as she opened her car door.

"Damn, woman" was the first thing Kaden said once the call had connected. "You could kill a man with that kind of tease."

"Well, I definitely don't want to kill you. Maybe I could

make it up to you in person?" She closed the car door as quietly as she could and headed toward his condo.

"I don't know if I'm going to be able to hold on until next weekend."

"Who said anything about next weekend? Check your front door."

"No way—"

Allie cut him off with a press of her thumb.

After tucking her phone into her purse, she smoothed her short dress down her thighs. Cass had tried to convince her she should wear a trench coat and nothing else, but Allie hadn't been comfortable with the idea. It felt too close to being messy in public. Instead, she'd worn a new red dress with a deep, plunging neckline that left no room for a bra and the same lace thong from the video.

Her heart was beating so hard, she worried it was going to crack her ribs. It was going to be okay. Kaden had said he wanted to give this a try. This was just her showing him how much effort she was willing to put into their relationship. That was all. Plus, he'd sounded excited before she'd cut him off.

The front door opened and there he was, wearing a soft gray T-shirt and jeans, his phone still clutched in one hand.

"Surprise," Allie said in a small voice.

A smile broke across his face, making her heart flutter.

"TOUCHDOWN! WOOO! YEAHHHH, BITCH!"

Allie's eyes went wide. "I'm so sorry. I didn't realize you had people over. I'm just going to go."

"Wait!" Kaden reached out and snagged her wrist before she could flee back to her car. "Just come inside, please."

"I don't want to interrupt. Maybe I could come back

later or tomorrow. You don't have to worry about me. I have a hotel room by the airport."

"Allie, stop." Kaden's warm hand cupped the side of her face, forcing her to look at him. "You're not interrupting and there is no way in hell I'm letting you stay in a hotel tonight. Not when getting you into my bed has been a constant fantasy of mine for the last two weeks."

"Only the last two weeks?" she asked weakly, trying for humor.

He chuckled before pressing a long kiss to her lips. "For much longer than that, but it's been pretty much constant since I got home from my trip. Come on."

Allie laced her hand in his and let him pull her into his house. They walked down a short corridor that opened up into a spacious living room dominated by a large flat-screen and an L-shaped sofa occupied by three men, their attention completely focused on the football game blaring from the tv.

"All right, time to get your asses to your own homes," Kaden called loudly as he punched a button on the TV. The screen went dark to a chorus of outraged groans.

"Kaden," Allie hissed, but he completely ignored her.

"Come on, man. It's the last quarter," pleaded a Korean guy around Kaden's age in a blue shirt with a stylized ram's head on the front.

Heat bloomed in Allie's cheeks, so hot she worried they might catch fire. "Kaden, why not let them finish the game?"

"Because who knows how long it will actually last." The speaker stood up from the couch and Allie's stomach dropped into her shoes. "Nice to see you again, Allie," said Markus, the CEO of Kaden's company.

Maybe there would be an earthquake. Not a big one that would cause destruction and death and send most of

California to the bottom of the ocean, but a little one. Just big enough to swallow Allie whole and put her out of her mortified misery.

"Jae, you live four houses down," Markus said, leaning over to playfully punch the Korean man's shoulder. "We'll just move to your place."

"Fine, but I'm taking these," the third man said. He was a broad-shouldered Mexican man wearing a different team's jersey. With a glare at Kaden, he gathered up two open bags of chips and a half-empty six-pack of beer.

"Take whatever you want. Just get out of my house."

Markus and Jae gathered up various drinks and snacks and started for the door. When Markus paused in front of Allie, she said in a low, strangled voice, "I'm so sorry."

"Don't be. I don't blame him a bit," Markus said with a wink. "See you Monday, Kaden."

"See ya, boss man."

Before the front door had even fully closed, Kaden was pulling Allie up a set of stairs. When they reached the landing, but before he could lead her through the doorway that probably led to his bedroom, she tugged on his hand and said, "Wait."

He turned around and looked at her.

"That. That, down there, was messy."

"What do you mean?" Kaden asked, cocking his head to the side.

"Those're your friends! The first impression they got of me was you kicking them out for a booty call. They're going to think I'm some sex-obsessed, controlling bitch."

"Oh, Allie." He cupped the side of her face. "They know me. They know I would never date a controlling bitch. There will be plenty of time for you to get to know them later. They'll understand and love you. Just like I do."

"You love me?"

"I've loved you ever since my date at prom left me for another guy and you 'accidentally' spilled fruit punch all down her white dress."

A small laugh escaped Allie, even as tears pricked the corners of her eyes. "I'd forgotten about that. I had to pay for her dry-cleaning bill out of my babysitting money, but it was totally worth it." She wrapped her arms around his neck. "I love you, too." The words were soft, but they were true. Even with the gap of years, he was still the funny, caring guy he'd always been. Who had always looked out of her and pushed her to try new things and been there when she'd fallen.

His mouth claimed hers hard, like he was trying to tell her how much those words meant with every press of his lips and lick of his tongue. And she kissed him back, just as fiercely.

When they both came up for air a while later, he grinned against her mouth. "Do you know what would have been messy?"

It took Allie's pleasure-addled brain a moment to parse his words and another to figure out what he was talking about. "What?"

He took her hand again and led her into his bedroom. The room was dominated by a large king-sized bed with a carved wooden headboard. The walls were painted gray and had no pictures or posters on them. Aside from a framed picture of him with his parents on the dresser, there really wasn't a lot of personality in the room. Allie guessed that he didn't spend a lot of time here except for sleeping.

"What really would have been messy," he continued as he moved behind her to unzip the back of her dress, "is if I'd not kicked them out and instead just bent you over the kitchen table."

Allie sucked in a breath as he slid the straps of her dress down her arms, his mouth pressing kisses into her exposed shoulders.

"If I'd just hiked up this dress to show them what a perfect pussy looked like. Let them hear those sweet little whimpers you make when I have my tongue deep in you." Her dress pooled at her feet and his hands cupped her exposed breasts. "Not that I would ever do that."

"Because that would be messy," she replied. His fingers gently pinched and rolled her nipples, making her arch her back.

"Because it would be very messy."

The idea made her blood race. The thought of Kaden's friends watching as he fucked her senseless was both thrilling and terrifying. Knowing that he'd never actually go through with it, because he'd promised, made the words, the fantasy, more delicious.

One hand went down to toy with the little pink bow on her panties. "Are these the same ones from the video you sent me?"

"Uh-huh." She would have said more, but his hand had moved on from the bow and was now fully cupping her pussy.

He let out an approving groan before slipping her thong down her thighs. "These will make an excellent addition to my collection."

"How many pairs of women's panties do you have in this collection?" Allie narrowed her eyes at him.

"Two." His hand came down on her ass with a smack. The unexpected sting of it forced a squeak from her. "Now, get on the bed. Hands and knees."

Allie hurried to comply and couldn't help but watch over her shoulder as he moved around the room. First, he quickly undressed and it struck Allie again just how perfect he was. His thick cock swayed as he pulled various items out of the drawer of the nightstand and set them on the top. A condom and lube.

The fact that he remembered made her heart warm. It was a small thing, but Kaden was a mishmash of so many amazing small things.

Then he pulled out a tablet.

"What's that for?"

"You'll see." He fiddled with the tablet for a minute before setting it up on top of the nightstand with the screen facing Allie and then climbed up behind her on the bed.

There was the sound of a wrapper tearing and then the pop of a bottle being opened. Fingers covered in cool, slick liquid slid over Allie's slit, moving up to tease her clit before plunging into her core. She let out a little cry and tried to work herself back on the fingers that kept a steady rhythm in and out of her.

Before she could get too worked up, though, the hand retreated and was replaced with the head of Kaden's cock at her entrance.

"Answer the call, Allie."

"What?" she asked, looking up from where she'd dropped her head onto the bedspread. Someone was trying to video call the tablet. She glanced over her shoulder to where Kaden had his phone out. "Oh!" She reached out and pressed the Accept Call button on the tablet. Kaden's face filled the screen, his grin wide and mischievous as always.

He'd muted both devices so that only video was being streamed between the two, not audio. She couldn't help but look back at him over her shoulder.

"Eyes forward," he said with another smack to her ass.

When she looked back at the tablet, Kaden had changed the angle on his phone so she could see herself bent over in front of him. It was a perfect view of the planes of his stomach, his cock thick and jutting toward her round ass. Had she always had those two little dimples at the base of her spine?

"This view is just too perfect not to share," he said as he used his free hand to guide the head of his cock through her folds.

That delicious, surreal feeling had returned. She could both watch and feel everything he was doing. She gave a little wiggle, rubbing herself along his cock and the ass, her ass, in the video wiggled as well.

Kaden moved the camera closer so she could watch as his cock spread her open and pushed slowly inside of her. Intense pleasure raced up her spine and made her flex her hands, bunching the bedspread between her fingers. When he was as deep into her as he could get, he let out a low "fuck" as his free hand came up to cup the curve of her hip.

He started a slow stroke in and out of her and Allie had a front-row view. The combination of feeling him stretching her open and watching it happen was better than anything Allie had ever experienced before.

"Fuck, how do you feel this good?"

Allie could only whimper and push herself back on his cock, meeting him stroke for stroke. Her breathing became quick and ragged as he increased his speed. Pleasure built in the pit of her stomach as he slammed into her over and over.

"Touch yourself. I need to feel you come on my dick again."

Her hand trembled slightly as she worked it down her body to find her clit. Everything was warm and slick and wet and she couldn't help dipping her fingers down to stroke along Kaden's shaft as he slid into and out of her.

"As good as that feels, it's not what I told you to do," Kaden growled out. He slammed into her and stayed deep, grinding with little swirls of his hips. Warm spikes of pleasure radiated from her core.

Her hand went to her clit and her slick fingers started making small, tight circles with just the right amount of pressure.

The view on the tablet shifted. The light wasn't as good, but Allie could see her fingers as they worked her clit. Just past them the shadows were thicker, but she could still make out Kaden's cock as it started fucking into and out of her once more. Every nerve in her body lit up, bracing itself for the peak to come. That sweet anxiety ratcheted up her body, making every limb quake and her breathing fall from her mouth in little thin pants.

"That's it, sweetheart. Come on my cock."

Allie tried to keep her eyes open, to watch herself do just that, but she couldn't. Her orgasm swept her under and all she could do was scream her release, her eyes tightly shut, one hand clenched in his bedspread, the other pressed against her clit, drawing it out as much as possible.

When the aftershocks had finally subsided enough for Allie to draw a full breath of air, she looked back up at the screen.

"You have no idea how amazing that was to watch, to feel. Goddamn, Allie."

Kaden had moved the camera again. This time she could see both his face and his hips as he started increasing his pace once more. The walls of her pussy were sensitive and aching from her climax and the feel of him pounding into her was almost enough to send her over the edge again.

She knew he was getting close by the way his muscles tensed. His hand kept squeezing her thigh, not enough to hurt, though she wouldn't mind if he left fingerprint bruises on her. A souvenir of sorts.

His pace turned fast and needy. The video on the tablet became shaky and then spun showing the side of the room and not Kaden at all as he let out of a low "fuck." She could feel him jerk inside her, his body curled over her back.

Hot, quick breath blew over her sweat-slicked shoulders. The hand that had been curled around her hip started stroking down her side. With his body caging her like that, she felt safe.

Eventually, he pulled out of her and rolled over on the bed with a groan. Allie pressed the End Call button on the tablet before crawling over to him. He gathered her close and pressed a kiss to her hair. Her ear was pressed to his chest, where she could hear his rapid heartbeat starting to slow down.

"Fucking hell, Allie. You can stalk me and interrupt my football game any time."

"Hey!" Allie raised her head, indignant. "I didn't stalk you."

"Oh yeah? Then how did you know where I lived?" The smile on his face was pure cheeky smugness.

"From the paperwork for the inappropriate and presumptuous gift *you* bought *me* after one night together."

His laugh was loud and made his chest vibrate under her. "Fair enough. Guess we'll just have to be creepy stalkers together then." His fingers slid her through her hair, brushing back from her face. He leaned in and pressed a soft kiss to her lips before moving her off his chest. "Let me go take care of this and I'll be right back," he said with a wave towards his crotch.

As Kaden disappeared into the bathroom, Allie couldn't help but lie on his bed and wonder at the chain of events that had led her here. To think that she owed her current state of blissed-out happiness to the world's most boring fish-based wedding speech.

On his way back in, Kaden turned off the lights and then helped Allie get under the covers. His body curled around her, one arm slung over her stomach. Her body was sated and relaxed, like it knew this was exactly where it was always meant to be.

"I'm really glad you changed your mind," Kaden said, his voice soft and full of emotion.

"Me too." If that ridiculous purple vibrator hadn't shown up, who knew if she'd ever have had the courage to try to make this work. A future without Kaden's laugh or dancing with him to jazz bands or all the dirty, amazing things he could do to her body? The thought of that bleak future made her shiver.

His arm tightened around her waist. "Keep that up and I'll have to fuck you again before we get some sleep."

"Who says I want to sleep now?" Allie teased with a purposeful wiggle of her ass. She could feel his cock stirring back to life behind her. "Besides, I didn't get a great view of the finale. Someone forgot they were holding a camera."

Kaden's breath caught as she reached behind her to cup his balls.

"I'll just have to make it up to you. Promise."

Allie couldn't help grinning. She knew Kaden. After way too long, he was hers, and he always kept his promises.

AFTERWORD

I hope you enjoyed Allie and Kaden's story as much as I enjoyed writing it.

If you'd like a free bonus spicy epilogue for these two, you can sign up for my newsletter, The Aviary. I will never sell your data and you can unsubscribe at any time.

Newsletter Sign Up

ABOUT THE AUTHOR

Nikki is a nerdy gal living her best life in Seattle with her partner and their pup. She enjoys crocheting, playing video games, and reading romances of all sorts. Her contemporary romances strive to be playful while containing a good helping of spice and all take place in the Pacific Northwest which she calls home.